GW00976218

TULLAMORE
LIONS CLUB

Published by Tullamore Lions Club
www.tullamorelionsclub.com

Text copyright © Dolores Keaveney 2024
Illustration copyright © Dolores Keaveney 2024
Artwork copyright © Dolores Keaveney 2024
All rights reserved

Written and illustrated by Dolores Keaveney
www.doloreskeaveney.com

Printed in Ireland by Print Plus, Tullamore, Co. Offaly
www.printplus.ie

ISBN 978-1-0687995-0-1

9 781068 799501 >

The Lions The Bees and The Bogs

President's Message

The Tullamore Lions Club is a voluntary, charitable organisation that has raised well in excess of €1.25m in recent years for worthy causes both locally and further afield.

The Club, as part of its sustainability agenda, recently initiated a bog restoration project on Clonbeale More Bog in Rath near Birr. Arising from this project, it was decided to spread the message of conservation in storybook format. This delightful publication, superbly written and illustrated by Dolores Keaveney, captures the essence of what the Tullamore Lions Club is attempting to convey to future generations.

We hope that the adventures of the Lion in an Irish bog will raise awareness of sustainable life practices and inspire today's youth to become guardians of the environment in future years.

Larry Fleming
President, Tullamore Lions Club

Once upon a time there lived a beautiful lion
on the grasslands and woodlands of Africa.
One day the lion had a visitor.
A magical bee just landed on its nose.

"Hello Lion," said the bee,
"how are you today?"

"I am very well," said the lion,
"but I am a bit bored here
and could do with a new adventure."

"Well I am just the right insect because I am
going on an adventure far away.
Would you like to come with me?" asked the bee.
"I will show you something beautiful
and I think you will enjoy it."

"Of course I would."
said the lion.

"There is just one thing that I have to do before we go," warned the bee.

"You are way too big to come with me as you are. I am a magical bee and have magical powers.

I will drop some magic pollen dust on your nose. I have it stored in the pollen basket on my leg. I promise I will not hurt you."

"Ok," said the lion. After all he had been in many big fights with other lions and large animals. Surely a tiny tip on the nose would not hurt and might be well worth it.

So the magical bee
dropped some pollen dust
onto the lion's nose.

Just like that, the
lion shrank down to
the size of the bee and
grew two big wings.

"That wasn't too bad,"
said the bee to the lion.
"That was easy,"
said the lion.

"Let's go, we have a very long journey ahead of us," said the bee.

So off they both flew.
They travelled for hours and hours until they came to their destination.

"What is this place called?" said the lion to the bee.

"This is a bog!" exclaimed the bee.
"What is that?" asked the lion.

So the magical bee told the beautiful lion all about bogs.

"This is a bog in Ireland called Clonbeale More Bog."

"A bog is land *that* is wet,
with soft brown soil called
peat underneath.

It is covered in mosses,
plants and pools of water.
It may look like solid land,
but is more like a spongy carpet!

This is because the peat contains nine
times more water than solid material.

The peat is made up of the plants
that have died and built up on top
of one another over thousands
of years.

Bogs are very special because they are very rare. They are home to vast amounts of biodiversity such as unusual plants and animals."

"What is biodiversity?" asked the puzzled lion.

"I am glad you asked." replied the clever bee.

"Biodiversity means all the different kinds of life that you will find in the bogs such as animals, fungi and bacteria. All the different species work together to maintain balance and support life there."

"Do you know how old a bog is?"
asked the bee.
"I have no idea," answered the lion.
"Let me explain," said the bee.

"This bog is about 8,000
to 12,000 years old.
It starts with a lake
which becomes overgrown.

The reeds and plants decay and
fall to the bottom of the lake.

Over the years moss grows over
all of this and the bog is born."

Bogs are one of the oldest landscapes.
They look almost exactly the same
as they did thousands of years ago.
They connect us with our past.

Without bogs we would lose amazing
plants like sundews, bog rosemary,
sphagnum mosses, bog cotton
and others.

We might also lose spectacular birds like
curlews, skylark, meadow pipit, snipe
and more.

Bog Rosemary is a rare and
special flower and is featured
on the Offaly county crest.

Bogs are also important places
where carbon is stored.

The mosses that grow in the
bogs absorb carbon.
This prevents it escaping
into the atmosphere.

The sphagnum moss changes into peat
and the peat can store the carbon
for thousands of years.

Clonbeale More Bog
is being conserved,
which means it is being looked after.

This helps prevent the carbon from
adding to global warming, which
affects everyone on the planet
and endangers all the flowers,
animals, birds and bees."

"Did you ever hear of an archaeologist?"
asked the bee.
"No I did not," replied the lion.

So the bee told the lion all about
the work of archaeologists in the bog.

"Archaeologists are people who study human history.
They love to visit bogs and they have discovered
many ancient objects in perfect condition.
This is because the bog peat helps to preserve them.

Swords, artifacts, old wooden items,
leather, shoes and lots of other
things have been found buried
deep in bogs."

"Wow," said the lion. "I love it here.
Can I run and jump and lie down
and roll in the bog?"
"You can do that if you wish,
but be very careful
where you jump.
You might just disappear
in the mucky bog.

Just one thing,
you are too small to jump...
one little drop of pollen
dust on your nose and
you will be back to your
usual size," said the bee.
"Thank you,"
said the lion.

So the magical bee dropped some pollen
dust on the lion's nose and suddenly,
the lion was back to its normal size.
Off he went, running and jumping
and rolling around the bog.

The lion let out a huge roar with delight. "Rrrrrrrrrrrrrr!"

They both stayed there for a long time
and saw the beautiful flowers and
spectacular birds that lived in the bog.
They also met some animals such
as a fox and its little babies.

"This has been a wonderful trip for me," said the lion to the bee. "It is great that bogs like this are being conserved."

"When I go back to Africa I will try to help others to take more care of our special habitats.

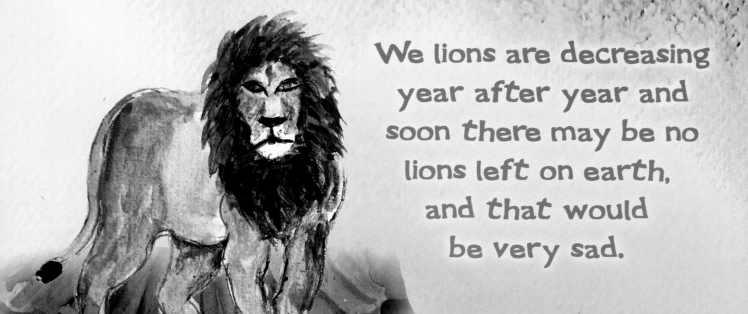

We lions are decreasing year after year and soon there may be no lions left on earth, and that would be very sad.

Without us lions our biodiversity would suffer.
There would be lots more plant eating animals
leading to overgrazing and causing the quality
of the water to become worse.

People would also suffer as well.
Without lions to keep manners on large
herbivores, their numbers and boldness
would increase and that would
be very bad for us all."

"Exactly," agreed the bee.
"The same applies to us bees."

Did you know that there are over 20,000 species of bees in the world and 99 species are in Ireland?

We are one of the most important creatures on the planet because we pollinate 80% of all flowering plants and most of the main human food crops.

Bees need to be treasured and looked after or there will be no seeds to grow crops."

Bees Are Very Important

1. Queen lays eggs

2. Nurse bees feed larvae

3. House bees seal Cells

drone cell

queen cell

worker cell

4. New bees

5. Youngest worker bees clean cells

6. Older worker bees forage

After a long happy day together,
the bee said to the lion,
"It is now time for
you to go back home
to Africa."

The bee dropped some pollen dust on the lion's nose.
The lion shrank down until he was the same size
as the bee again and off they went.

Many hours later they were back in the lion's habitat.
One last trickle of pollen dust on the nose
and the lion was back to his normal self.

"That was a wonderful adventure,"
said the lion to the bee.

"There can be lots more
adventures in the future
if you would like that"
promised the bee.

"Yes, I would like that
very much," replied the lion.
"Great," said the bee,
"I will be back soon."
The bee waved its magical
wings and off it flew.

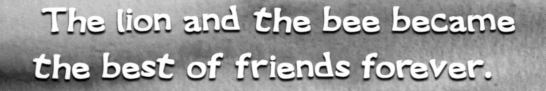

The lion and *the* bee became
the best of friends forever.

I wonder did *the* lion ever return
for another adventure?

What do you *think?*

Bog Rosemary is a rare
and special flower and is
featured in the Offaly
County Crest.

Clonbeale More bog is one of many privately owned bogs around Ireland. These bogs are beautiful to look at and you can find some interesting plants and animals living there. However, they are not in a healthy state, and many of the species in these bogs are declining. As these bogs were drained in the past, they are emitting large amounts of Carbon Dioxide into the atmosphere which is damaging our climate.

In 2023, Clonbeale Peatland Conservation Group set about conserving the very important bog. Firstly, we found a bog expert whom we asked to carry out a detailed study on Clonbeale More. The result was a detailed conservation plan. This plan recommended a number of measures to stop the decline in Clonbeale More Bog. In 2024 Offaly County Council provided the funds to enable the conservation measures to be completed.

Once completed, Clonbeale More will stop emitting large amounts of Carbon Dioxide thus helping our Climate. Plant and animal species in Clonbeale will benefit and some that were previously lost will return. As a result, Clonbeale More will be a wonderful place to visit in the future where we can all learn more about nature.

Sunset at
Clonbeale More

Acknowledgements

Tullamore Lions Club would like to thank the following.
Without their creativity, help and support this book would not
have been possible.

Dolores Keaveney, a wonderfully talented author and artist.
Dolores was inspired to write this beautiful story and to accompany it with
stunning illustrations that bring the book to life.

Friends and family, for taking the time to read drafts of the book and for
their suggestions, encouragement, and support.

Offaly County Council and Creative Ireland for their guidance and generous funding.

Lorraine and Anthony and all on the Print Plus team
who contributed to producing a book of the highest quality.

Testimonials

I loved this story. Every child loves to have
a story read aloud and this one grabs the
attention of all ages. I loved the simplistic
explanations throughout and the beautiful
illustrations, but also the more in-depth details
about bogs and how they are formed.
It is important for children to know and

understand these things and I think it is explained fantastically well in
this book. It gives children a sense of looking after the environment, which is
also very important. I thoroughly enjoyed it!
Grainne read this book to her 3 cousins, Darcy (7), George (5) and Marcus (3).

Grainne Walsh
Team Ireland Boxer and Paris 2024 Olympian from Tullamore

~~~~~~~~~~~~~~~~~~~~~~~~~~~~~~~~~~~~~

This book is a lovely, very enjoyable read.
It is just perfect for its target audience and the explanations are thorough.

Muireann Kenneally, aged 12, St. Ciaran's N.S.

~~~~~~~~~~~~~~~~~~~~~~~~~~~~~~~~~~~~~

This beautifully illustrated children's book is a lovely introduction to the
importance of biodiversity, particularly highlighting the unique ecosystems of our
bogs. The narrative is engaging and easy to understand, making it perfect for
young readers. The book emphasizes the need to protect our natural
resources and the diverse species that call them home. A great resource
for any Primary School library/classroom.

Kay Joyce, Principal, St Colman's N.S., Mucklagh